Not a Day of Miracles

brief stories

David Macpherson

Not a Day of Miracles: brief stories
Copyright 2020 by David Macpherson

Cover photo by Gary Hoare
GaryHoare.com

macphersondavid607@gmail.com
David Macpherson is a Writing Stuff is his Facebook page.
Find him at instagram at davidscottmacpherson
He blogs at 100pagedash.wordpress.com

Wing Mending

Every year on VE day, it is my task to take my grandfather down to Atlantic City to blow his veteran's pension on blackjack and the craps tables. It doesn't take long. The cocktail waitresses flirt with his slow-moving hands and generous tips.

He tells them that he flew for the RAF, that's the Royal Air Force to you, my dear. And when he says flew, he does not mean the cowardly way of being encased in an airplane but flew. Really flew with wings. Fought the Nazis like birds, like superior birds. Part of a little-known hush-hush group called Lord Stanley's Winged Reconnaissance Group. They flew with canvas wings. They were used for covert actions, when planes were too cumbersome. They saved many a neck for England and the Allies. They would have been knighted, if they were allowed to admit their existence.

The cocktail waitresses smile broadly, pat his hand, and no doubt water down his next drink. This time, a waitress takes me aside. "Is he for real?" she asks. "I never heard of anything like that before."

I tell her that my grandfather would show me a worn, folded photograph of young British soldiers on a beach fixing large canvas wings. In the background looks like men flying in the air like kites. On the back, in my grandfather's hand, is written, "Me and the boys in Dover doing a spot of Wing Mending. 1944."

She asks, "Can I see that picture?"

I tell her I don't bring it. I don't show it. That everyone who sees it tries to find the fault. Everyone explains about photo manipulation and what computers can do, even make something this fake look real. I tell her it's just not worth the conversation or conjectures.

She does not understand. She asks, "So do you believe it? Do you think it's real?"

After the pension money is gone, Grandfather orders me to push his chair to the boardwalk. To watch the breakers and see the pretty girls in bikinis. He gets out of his chair, leans on his cane and watches with avid attention. But soon I spy him looking at the seagulls dancing on the horizon. The drunk but perfect dips and circles. The navigation of air currents and want. And grandfather shakes his head dismissively at the distant birds.

"They're doing it wrong," he says. "It's all wrong."

Sleeves

The god she worshiped was pierced and had full sleeves of tattoos. "The whole story of creation is on his arms. From the Fall, to Flight, to the Halfway House of Salvation. It's on his skin. Except for one piece, by his left elbow, a blank oval, like an egg. That's the secret. That's the truth he ain't telling. That piece, alright? That's the part we pray to." She let go of my arm and stared at my skin, my canvas. She focused on the parts with no tattoos. She stared at my untouched pieces, looking for something unspoken.

Several Ways to Woo a Lady with the Aid of a Ball Peen Hammer

Defend the lady's honor by brandishing the hammer against would be suitors not as acceptable as yourself.

Bang out a jaunty drumbeat on a nearby drainpipe for her musical enjoyment.

Smash coffee cups when her drink arrives with too much cream and sugar.

Subdue marauding rats gone mad from eating fermented refuse and are nipping at the hem of her skirts.

If wrapped in a crimson bow with a few lines of Keates engraved on the shaft, the ball peen hammer makes an excellent token of endearment.

Pound down large piles of horse droppings so they may not offend her view of the landscape.

Place the hammer through your button hole and wear it instead of a flower and she will think your cutting edge commitment to style most becoming.

The glare of the sun hitting its polished head will distract white slavers, allowing her easy escape.

It may be bartered at the market for a parcel of shortbread biscuits if she appears peckish and of need of nourishment.

With it you can vanquish gnomes, redcaps, and dyspeptic theater critics to ensure her fine disposition.

Honestly be able to state that though Lord Hallingford cuts a stately figure, he does not carry a ball peen hammer.

Juggling with a nectarine, a skein of yellow dyed wool and a ball peen hammer is a delightful spectacle, thoug

h it should be noted that sleight of hand tricks with the hammer must be omitted from the repertoire.

The simple act of grasping the handle will make you giddy with confidence, feeling for once like a proper man

Breaking Down Lions

There is a girl with a wrench who disassembles lions. Most times, she sits on the side of the hill shredding grass blades. Looking up at the pastel candy clouds. But sooner than a daydream can reach fruition, she will sense the clanking of a metal lion approaching her from the path below.

A lion, tarnished by rains and dented by the hunt. Its heat shielding will be missing from its flank and a rear leg will drag behind it like an anchor due to frozen ball bearings. With labor, it will find itself by the girl with the wrench, lower its head upon her lap and let its processors hiss surrender.

She will stroke its profile until the rust flecks away onto the current. She will take her wrench and unburden the lion into parts. Every piece, bolt, screw, belt put neatly into piles. Nothing out of place. Nothing missing, except for the lion itself.

All that remains will be the head, with the servo processor still glowing the amber eyes. The girl will stare into them and hush the fear she sees in its fading gaze. With pliers stolen from her older sibling, Sister Left Hand, she will remove the sharp teeth one by one from the lion's jaw. Some teeth will be caked in old oxidized blood. Soon it will be toothless.

The girl with the wrench will speak. My Sister Left Hand made you. I am sure you can tell me legends of rended flesh and prey trembling neath sparse cover, but you are here with me now and you purr into pieces so valiantly. You came to me because it felt right and just. My younger Sister Right Hand will steal your parts when I sleep and make you new. There will be no more conflict, only rebirth. That's all I can promise you. Rebirth. Nothing more, nothing less than that.

Behind and above the girl with the wrench, will be the sound of metal wings, thin as gossamer, circling the air. The reworked creations of Sister Right Hand. One can almost sense the pride in the new forms. See, the girl with wrench will say, see what you can become.

But by then, the amber eyes of the lion will be deadened to blackout curtains. And the girl will put the last relic into a pile, regain her poise, stare into the sky, try to find familiar faces in the space between the clouds.

An Incident at a Naomi Fein Slumber Party

It was after making popcorn and setting up Naomi's bedroom for all four of the girls to sleep when Bree found the Ouija board in the closet. "Let's find out what the spirits are up to," Bree said as she arranged the girls around the board. They all put their fingertips on the indicator and it immediately jumped around making fast circles around the board. The room exploded with accusations of, "Are you moving it?"

The indicator stopped suddenly and then shot out to letters. Tam sounded out each letter and then figured the words out. "Let's see. It all spells out this: is he here? In the room. Is he here?"

Bree said, "Oh spirit. There are no men here. Just the four of us. Are you confused?"

The board spun around, twisting the girls' fingers and found the letters again. "I am not the one confused. I am not a spirit. I am a Ouija board. There is no ghost, just me the board."

Jilly turned to Naomi, "That's interesting. The medium of communication is actually the one that talks. It seems very post-modern."

Naomi said, "What's post-modern?"

Jilly said, "I'm not sure. I read it in an article to help me with a book report. It sounds good though."

Tam shushed them as the indicator moved. She spoke for the Ouija board. "Is he here? My boyfriend. I have a great sleek guy, but he is been so cold. He hardly talks to me."

Naomi asked, "Who is he?"

Tam watched the letters pointed out and said, "He's the Magic Eight Ball who is in your brother's room. He says he lives in the sock drawer. Can you get him? He won't answer my calls."

The girls looked at Naomi, who thought of the request with all the deep concern she had. She nodded approval and Jilly ran out of the room, coming back soon with a black plastic ball draped in a tube sock. The sock was thrown into the hallway and Naomi assigned roles. Jilly would speak for the Eight Ball. Tam continued her role with the Ouija board and Bree asked the questions that needed to be asked. Naomi would lord over the proceedings; it was her room after all.

Bree said, "Oh Ouija board, your great love is here. We have him next to you."

The Ouija board sped out letters and words, practically babbling. "Oh honey, you are here. I am so happy. I missed you so much. You have not gotten in touch with me. I've been trying to reach you, but I have not heard a word. Is something wrong?"

The indicator stopped. Naomi nodded towards Jilly, who shook the Eight Ball and then read what appeared in the little window. "My sources say no."

The Ouija board continued, "So nothing is wrong, but why have you remained so quiet?"

The Magic Eight Ball was shaken and said, "Reply hazy try again."

The Ouija Board stuttered to the next few letters. "Okay, you want me to speak clearer. I get it. You always want me to be precise. Let me try it again. Are we in trouble as a couple?"

Jilly shook and read, "My reply is no."

The Ouija board rushed out, "Good. I was so worried. I'm sure you were busy, but dear, why can't you communicate more? Don't you like talking with me?"

The Magic Eight Ball came up with, "As I see it yes."

"But you are so silent, you let me prattle on and then you do not get back to me, making me worry that you do not love me. You still like the time we have, do you not?"

"Outlook good," he said.

The Ouija board said, "What is it then? Is it your mother, the crystal ball? I know she does not approve of me."

The Magic Eight Ball said, "Better not tell you now."

"I knew it. But you are a grown man. You do not need to listen to her. I thought you want to have a life with me? Don't you want to spend the future with me?"

"Most likely," Jilly read from the Magic Eight Ball.

Tam looked at Naomi, "The words seem like she's shouting at him, Naomi, so should I shout?"

Naomi shook her head, "My mom probably wouldn't like it. Let's just pretend that she is speaking in a quiet voice."

Tam said, "Okay, here goes. The board says, this is not fair of you. I give. I keep giving. You just hang out with the boy oriented toys in the sock drawer and will not tell me what I can do. Why will you not just tell me what you are feeling?"

"It is certain."

The Ouija board took a while to reply. "What does that mean? What is certain? I just need you to be certain for once. Is that too much? I just cannot stand it. It is certain. You never tell me what you mean." The indicator raised up, pushing the girls' arms over their heads. It spun like a top and flew into the pillows at the top of the bed.

Bree leaned over, picked up a corner of the pillow. "It's in there, shaking. I think she's crying, as much a plastic pointer can cry."

Tam looked at Jilly. Jilly shook the Magic Eight Ball and read what showed up in the window, "Women, am I right?"

Naomi left the room and returned with her dad's hammer. She smashed the Eight Ball into little pieces and mopped up the liquid with a towel.

The Loud and the Silence

In the beginning there was the megaphone, orange like a citrus galaxy. This was before star time. Now, was only the megaphone. But there was no one to shout into it. There was nothing to amplify. No breath to bring forth a joyful noise. The megaphone felt itself hollow. Certainly it felt hollow, but this feeling was more than a coring out of space. This was a stood up at the bar all night and waiting for the phone to ring hollow.

Then the megaphone amplified its desire and Princess Bird Girl appeared. She was not basked in absolute perfection, but she was the first amplification and must be thought of as an early, though seminal work. A decent first try. Consider Princess Bird Girl as the crayon portrait adhered to the fridge door of creation. Primitive, but necessary. There was nothing of color in her, not even in her chicken legs. Her pinafore was perfectly tied with the precision of a freeway cloverleaf traffic jam. Her crown, of course she had a crown, she was a princess and all princesses must have crowns. Her crown was cut from left over gold wrapping paper.

So let it begin. Let Princess Bird Girl approach the megaphone in the middle of the eggshell void. Let her pick it up with two small feathery hands. Let her place its short end to her lips and as she feels the touch of electricity as all ordained first kisses generate, let her hold it to her lips for an eternity. As she thinks of the correct first word to be amplified.

And Princess Bird Girl said that word "Hello." And it flew out of the megaphone and repeated itself in the void. Hello Hello Hello. And nothing else. Then she thought that was the wrong word. The void does not want a greeting. But a statement of purpose. She picked up the megaphone and said the right word. She said, "Echo." And the universe reverberated echo echo echo. And from the megaphone came a branch of the first tree. And as the word echo bounced around the void, the branch continued to push out of the megaphone. And on the branch was a black bird.

Emboldened, Princess Bird Girl shouted more words out. Like Louder. Faster. Bigger. Rounder. Feedback. Oscillate. Din. Cacophony. Tinnitus. And from the amplification an orchard fell out of the megaphone with Princess Bird Girl shouting out like a preacher of a mosh pit tent revival.

The Orchard took with stately red humming fruit that sounded like an orchestra tuning up or a formula one racer revving at the starting line. And the back bird took one of the fruit in his claws and flew up into the void and dropped it and it exploded into a riot of sound and when the ruckus settled, there were the stars and chamber music.

The black bird dropped another fruit and from it came the oceans and fado. The third fruit the bird dropped created punk rock and the mountains. The fourth gave us opera arias and the women to sing them. The fifth fruit gave up the blues and the men to suffer through them.

And when the world was alive and aloud the black bird turned its wing and flew into silence. And princess Bird Girl put down the megaphone and heard all the traffic and left out the side door into silence. And the untended orchard went fallow and settled into silence.

But the megaphone is still here. Waiting. Like an amplifier seconds before sound check with a question burning on its unmoving mouth, "Can you hear me? Can you hear me? Am I loud enough? Can you hear me? People in the back, can you hear me now

Traffic Signs You Might Come Across

Stop Sign - Make sure your vehicle comes to a complete stop. Check to see if it is clear before reinstating movement.

Yield Sign - If the road you are entering is clear, you may proceed without any adjustment. If the road is occupied, cease movement until you can safely enter the flow of traffic.

Slow Children Sign - This is an area where children live and might run into the street so you must slow your speed and drive cautiously.

Rock Slide Sign - Dive with caution due to the possibility of rocks impeding your way.

Exploding Road Sign - Drive with caution due to the possibility that the damned rebels have mined the road.

Solid Double Lane Lines - Under no circumstance can you pass the car in front of you.

Perforated Lane Lines - You may pass the car in front of you if there is no traffic coming from the opposite direction.

Solid Double Lane Lines with Red Arrows in the Middle - If safe, you may fire bomb the car in front of you.

Ped X-ing - Stop your car if a pedestrian is in the walkway and allow them to cross completely.

Ped XX-ing Sign - Accelerate your car if a pedestrian is in the walkway. It is not proper to back up if you miss, please follow logical rules of the road.

No Hitchhiker Sign - If you pick up a hitchhiker in this designated area, you will be fined.

No Hostage Sign - If you pick up a hostage in this designated area, you will be fined. It should be clarified that you are allowed to have a hostage you previously obtained, but you are prohibited from taking any new ones.

No Littering - There is a fine for throwing trash from the car onto the road.

No Dumping - There is fine for throwing a body, dead or otherwise, from a car onto the side of the road. You won't see this sign much anymore, because it is felt that a no littering sign should take care of this as well.

Toll Ahead Sign - Slow your car and prepare to pay the assigned fee to use the next stretch of road.

Tribute Ahead Sign - Slow your car and prepare to pay the assigned tribute to the local warlord or overseer. You should know the price of the tribute before traveling, be it gold, diamonds, wheat or transplantable kidneys. It is your responsibility as a good driver to know this and other rules of the road.

Leaders

The hitchhiker slammed the trunk closed and walked over to the driver's window and framed his big face there. "Couple of things," he said, "you do have a spare tire back, but its old and shot. Be better to drive on no tire than that one.

The driver slapped the steering wheel. "I knew I should have got it replaced. Thought I was saving myself some money. And of course there is no cell reception out here."

The hitchhiker nodded. "Nother thing. There appears to be the dead body of a President of the United States folded up in your trunk."

The driver shook her head slowly, like she was keeping time to a mid tempo waltz. "Again?" she said. "This happens more than I would like to say." The hitchhiker shrugged. "Well," the driver said impatiently, "Which one is it."

"Which one is what," the hitchhiker asked.

The driver leaned toward the window. "Which president is in the trunk?"

The hitchhiker nodded, "I'm not entirely certain, but I believe that it was Millard Fillmore, our 13th President."

The driver stuck out her bottom lip like a child told that there will be no dessert, "He wasn't even a good one."

The hitchhiker patted her hand. "To be fair," he said, "he seems devoid of any vestigial presidential charisma, what with him crumpled in a ball by your tire iron and the bottle of windshield wiper solution."

"Most people are," she agreed. "I never get the good ones showing up dead in my trunk. I get Polk. Or Harrison. I get James Garfield so often I refuse to count. Had Nixon last month. He did open up trade with China, but does that make him good? I kind of doubt it.

"But do I get Lincoln?" she asked with head directed to the car roof. "Do I get Washington? What lucky trunk gets the moldering remains of

FDR? Wouldn't that be a fine change of pace? Having FDR dead in my trunk? I don't ask for much."

"What do you do with them? These bad dead presidents?" the hitchhiker asked.

"Well I don't throw them into a dumpster if that's what you're wondering. Just because James Buchanan, say, was a terribly ineffective administrator who brought on the Civil War as much as any one man could, he was still the President and deserves a proper burial. I toss him and all the other Presidents in my trunk in the compost heap at my Uncle's farm. In a couple years, no matter how awful a President they were, they are now equipped to help tomatoes grow to their finest potential as high grade organic fertilizer."

The hitchhiker nodded. "You know what we should do? We should just drive. On the flat tire. Just drive."

The driver looked ahead at the vanishing road, "But can't we break an axel or something bad?"

The hitchhiker smiled, "This car? Not this car. This car was built to go forward. I don't know where it's going, but do you think a tire is going to stop it?"

The driver turned the key and the engine took. "This is a bad idea. But when did that ever stop anyone. Get in. We got miles to burn and a President to toss in a compost pile. There is no time to waste."

Freeze Tag with Jack

Even then, I didn't like freeze tag. It is a baby's game. Pretending to be frozen after being tagged got old fast. We used to play real games: touch football, softball, or even volley ball when the park workers remembered to put up the net. But that year, around the time school started again, all anyone wanted to play was freeze tag.

It was because of the new kid, Jack. He didn't go to our school. Maybe he wasn't even from our development. He just showed up to play. He was small and blonde. Very blonde. Like white.

Jack was the master of being It. When he froze you, you stayed froze. Really frozen. You couldn't move. Your joint and muscles would rust and there you would stay until the game was over. When he tagged all of us, and he always did, then we would all be able to move again. If he tagged you in mid-leap, you would crash to the ground, still stuck in the same position when he touched you.

I hated it. If we were going to do freeze tag, it should be in the normal way. If I was going to be frozen, I wanted to be immobile by my own power, by willing myself to not move. I didn't need the help of something beyond my grasp.

One day in October, I went up to Jack before the game started. I said to him, "Hey, you know for this game, can't you not freeze us for real? Can't we just pretend to be frozen?"

Jack looked at me with his blue eyes and said, "That not how the game is played. It is played the right way, like a force of nature. Just as leaves turn to brown on the branch, certain rules must occur."

He laughed then and it wasn't a funny laugh. His eyes got less blue. And they were old. He smiled that not funny smile and said, "Hey, guess what? I'm It."

He shot his hand out and slapped down on my shoulder. My bones became strata. My muscles were glaciers. I breathed slowly like tundra. The game hadn't even begun and I was surely stuck.

After the game, Jack didn't release me. I was left there. Birds landed on my raised arm, like it was a perch. My parents had to bring me home with a hand cart. They kept me in the basement. Waiting for the Spring Thaw felt like forever

Millennium Locks

I was still drunk when the locksmith got to my apartment door. I said, "Thank God you're here. Can't get into my place. Key's not working."

The locksmith sniffed out the issue and said, "You sure you go the right key?"

"Fuck you," I said all polite. "I'm lit, but check it, I got only one key on the chain. Can't screw that up. I'm a one key guy, for just such an emergency. But today, no dice."

The locksmith shrugged so high the tools in his box rattled. "Let me take a look." He grabbed my key without asking and turned on his mag light to check out the lock. He stared for a bit and then whistled. "Well sir," he said acting proper and contract correct, "this ain't a problem I can fix. Actually this ain't even a problem. This is a product doing what it's supposed to do. You got yourself a Millennium Lock in there."

"What does that mean?" I asked.

The locksmith looked confused, "Sir. You got a Millennium Lock. You don't get that product by mistake. You pay extra for it; its something you know about."

"I wasn't the first tenant. I kept the apartment after my girlfriend went to Portland to follow this bassist. It was her apartment, then it was ours, not it's mine."

"Not anymore, sir. It's not anyone's anymore. You have a Millennium Lock. Don't you know them?" I just gazed at him. He waited, shrugged and went on. "They sell a specific product. It's a hell of a lock, works perfectly, tight system, strong tumblers. Works like a dream for a thousand times. After a thousand times of locking and unlocking, it freezes up for good."

"Freezes up for good? Is that a malfunction?"

The locksmith said, "No. It's designed that way. It's marketed that way. After a thousand times, you won't get into your apartment. Nothing is going to open it. People who get this installed know this. After a thousand lockings and unlockings, you got to move."

"Wait. I'm not getting in? That's crazy. Can't you do something?"

"No," the locksmith said. "It's done. You got to move."

"What about my stuff? How can I get my stuff?"

The locksmith paused for a bit and then said, "From what I hear, it's gone. In a week, the lock will be missing and the door open. Go into the place then and its empty."

"Empty? Where's the stuff? Where'd it go?"

"I don't know, sir. It's just gone. The place will be empty and pristine clean, like part of your stuff was your dirt and stains. Landlords don't have to paint for the new tenant, its so clean, they love it."

I said, "I need my stuff."

"You just think you do. I've seen this before. You get to leave here with nothing. Start over. Do something new. Do the same shit again. Whatever. No matter what, you ain't getting in here." The locksmith straightened up to his full height. He pulled his jacket straight and gave me a bill for a hundred dollars.

"For what?" I said. "You did nothing here."

"That's right. And for that honor, you owe me a hundred bucks."

I paid him and left the building before he did. I was still walking soft from the booze and I couldn't think of anyone who could help me. Who could stretch out a hand to me? I was homeless and drunk.

I finished the night riding the subway, not sleeping it off. I thought of the new place I now needed. I thought of the things I would fill it with. I also allowed myself to think of the front door of the new place I didn't have yet. The one thing I was sure of was the brand of lock I would insist for the door. That, at least, was something I could be certain of.

The Church of the Frankenstein Monster

They opened the church in downtown, in the space that once was Nelson's Hardware Store. The awning still reads, Established 1909. But now it is the Church. The official sign says they are the Church of the Son of God Made by Man. Though everyone knows it is the Church of the Frankenstein Monster. Their savior writ large.

No candles burn in any sconces. There is no flame. They have a synthesizer playing loud gothic organ music, but no one sings along. No one speaks. All those present act like they are unfamiliar with their own tongues, as if they were not their own. The facilitator stands in front holding a small van der graft generator in his outstretched hands. Sparks dance in their glass cage. Everyone's hair is on end. People seek salvation in the electricity. And that is almost the entirety of the service.

The man up front is not minister or priest. There is no true leader. He is thought of the facilitator, and nothing more. People in town, call the church heads Igors. That of course is said by those not of the church.

It's not hard to tell a believer from a tourist. The believers wear necklaces with small iron windmill blades on them. The faithful have tattoos of scarred stitching around both their wrists. It is the DIY stigmata of regeneration. The orthodox followers actually will cut themselves and sew up the wounds, giving themselves real scars, but this church is strictly Reform, and tattoos will suffice.

It is not the usual congregation you might see at a Baptist, or Lutheran and or even an Unitarian church. This is for those who felt molded by hands not their own. The lost come here. The broken. The angry. The ones who have rebuilt themselves from parts. The piercing fanatics. The plastic surgery junkies. The ones with burn wounds hidden beneath layers of clothing. The cutters. The recovering alcoholics who still dream of whisky. They find solace here in a place that worships a creature of god who was made by man.

If you stay to the end, you will see all of them pushed up from their seats as if by centrifugal force . They will spasm and dodge. You can smell the reverent blessings coming from this crazy quilt people, these raggedy souls, this hope for monsters blessed into beatific splendor. And en masse they will raise up their throats to heaven shout out praise with a loud guttural inarticulate scream of joy. A blasphemous hallelujah that will force the Gods to weep.

Artistic Necessity

Every Sunday, we children of Stiennerplatz would run out of church as soon as the final note of the last hymn was sounded, so we could hurry to the shore of the lake to draw.

It was Johanne, the go-getter, who discovered the sand outcropping by Beaver Boulder, where our model would make his appearance. We would be sitting with our sketch pads on our laps when the water before us would eddy and bubble. The lake was a cold swirling cauldron when at last our model would pop his green scaly head out of the water. He would tower over us, five meters, with his saucer eyes, trout mouth, yellow antenna: our model.

He was the most interesting sea serpent one was ever allowed to draw and draw we would. Our model only could stay above the water for a half hour, so we would draw with furious strokes. Near the end of the allotted time, we showed him our pictures. He leaned over and nudged the sides of those whose drawings he liked. The pleased nudge of a sea serpent was better than any accolade or grade ever could be.

Every week we would draw the serpent and we all grew as artists. But little Piotr grew too much. He began to experiment with flattening perspective, making the serpent almost a cubist creation. Piotr showed the serpent his most abstract portrait at the end of one drawing session.

Piotr beamed with pride. The sea serpent stared at the sketch pad for some time, and then bent over and swallowed Piotr in one gulp. Those of us who remained learned a valuable lesson. Cubism and abstraction is not good art.

We learned other lessons over the weeks.

After Henrietta was consumed, we learned to avoid allegorical drawings. Brunos's demise taught us to eschew hyper-realism. Pop commercialism became verboten with the loss of Hannah Bea.

Our dwindling band learned simple realism was the best and the safest of art, but our professor was not done teach us his gentle lessons.

When foreshortening was poorly done, or if the shading was clumsy we would lose a finger, for bad technique should never be ignored, but nipped in the bud.

We also learned not to criticize the sea serpent's teaching style when Johanne, the go-getter of the group, threw down his pad one day.

"Dull! Dull! Dull!" Johanne shouted. "You are turning us into plain bland artists. We are not inventive. We are safe. There is no spark in any thing we do. You are making us nothing but rudimentary craftsmen who's work can only be hung in dark smoky taverns." I thought the sea serpent looked mournful as he bit into Johanne.

And so I stand before you as the first and only graduate of this peculiar art academy. I am quite successful, having work in galleries in Bonn, Munich and Lisbon. My art adorns many a den and dining room. I have few sales to museums, but what do they know of art?

And I have critics; they call me pedestrian and unoriginal. The most vocal of critics, I invite to travel with me to Stiennerplatz, where they can meet my staunch supporter, my first and best instructor.

Let them explain their complaints to him.

Poetry Night

It is poetry night here and the next one goes to the stage area, adjusts the microphone and begins:

"Sometimes all I do is run on the wheel

Run on the wheel

Run on the wheel

The maze I'm in snakes and turns

Turns and snakes

And there is no cheese at the end brother

As I run on the wheel run on the wheel run on the wheel"

As the poet goes on 2 old timers in the back fidget. One of them twitches his nose, and says "Man running on a wheel. Lost in a maze. I've never heard that before." The second old timers laughs "Yeah, quite original." The old timers, wrapped in the undisclosed metaphor of their tails, try not to be bored by this new rodent poet on stage.

It is poetry night at the rat lab. The lab techs and the doctors are gone for the day, all the cages have been jimmied open, and the open mic list is over filled, which is fine because the featured reader couldn't make it, he was just given a shunt for the upcoming cosmetic trial and had to cancel. The next poet on the list bounds up and starts with passion:

"I am test tube slide specimen.

I am behavior modification.

I am this pellet makes you sleepy

This pellet makes you dead.

I am injections I am infections

I am the all the colors of dejection"

The first old timer turns and says, "What the hell is he talking about. He's in the control group. He's fine! Control groupies irk me. I hate goth rats from the suburbs acting like they are a vivisected stump." His companion says, "Oh you're not bitter." The two quietly laugh in their paws.

Soon enough, the second old timer is called up and does the latest of his open letter poems:

"Dear Revlon,Thank you for making me the rat I am today
The glow in the dark kind. My career path was cloudy till you came
Now all my friends look at me, see me with new eyes
Those that still have eyes.
I might have just been skulking about a alley all my days
But with you I went from pet store to lab cage to OR
To skinner box to rat maze to thesis paper to trash can
Who needs price line when I have you?"

The old timer is pleased. It got laughs in the right places. He would be hearing snapping fingers of approval if any of his audience had opposable thumbs.

The good feeling in the room is broken by the next reader, one of the hell with craft lets only talk about politics type poets. He goes:

" I know you lobbies think you are the victims here
And not the problem, and that's why you are the problem
You are too much victim. Are you rats or lemmings
Nothing but lemmings running the wheel, hitting the lever
Lost in the maze. You are the placebo of change
You are the negative return of injustice
Rats would flee this sinking ship
But for you lemming, the water is over you head and cold."

The first old timer scoffs. " Jesus, that's fine anger, but if he actually checked, he'd find he too is a rat, locked in a rat lab." The second says "Yeah I know our existence is bleak, I don't need him to remind me if he doesn't have a solution ."

The reading progresses into other poets other poems. One is about the pride the reader has in being clean and sober for three months. He didn't pull the morphine lever today and with the help of a higher power he won't pull the lever tomorrow. Another reads of celebrating his sexuality and of the love that dares not speak its name. You know,

Muskrat Love. The first old timers sighs "Another poetry reading. Tell me. Why do we do this every week. Does it make any difference?" The second says, "Of course it does. Because it is ours. What else feels so correct and true. What else are we truly allowed to be but poets. All of us." The first old timer, expecting no other answer, nods acceptance.

And now with the evening ending the host closes the reading by doing a poem himself. He chooses a cover poem he closes with almost every week. Something by Billy Corgan.

"The world is a vampire, sent to drain

Secret destroyers, hold you up to the flames

Despite all my rage I am still just a rat in a cage

Despite all my rage I am still just a rat in a cage

This is familiar to all, perhaps too familiar. But everyone mouths the words to the poem like liturgy. Even the old timers. All in one voice. Despite all my rage I am still just a rate in a cage. It gives them courage , as these moments are meant to, it gives them the strength to face the future hovering before them. To withstand a fate that is unknowing, vast and always approaching.

At the Slush Pile Saloon

A prose poem walked into a flash fiction bar and ordered a Vodka Gimlet. The bartender, a Faulkner-esque run-on sentence, didn't even twitch a comma; he just got out the booze and started making the magic. The regulars, down on their luck rejection magnets of various genres, were past annoyed at this guy coming in and drinking their liquor.

A six hundred word crime story, with a gin blossom nose and an obvious plot twist, sniffed, "Whatcha doing here with your fancified aires and inconclusive endings, like I want to wind up in an unread academic journal or in some entry level college anthology. No sir, not us."

A four hundred word modern fable sipping at his Guinness said, "Actually, I wouldn't mind showing up in one of those kinds of books. My kids wouldn't be ashamed of me if I was included in a course syllabus. Maybe I could see my grandkids with my head up high. They're just drabble fiction now, but you know kids, they grow fast and before I know it, they'll be as large as fantasy trilogies."

The crime story shouted at his compatriot, "No you don't. Don't say such rot. We ain't no puzzler that no one can understand if they're honest with themselves. No. We are working class, hard living populist gold. We are the backbone of literature. We got beginning, middle and ends. We got character development. We got punctuation where it's supposed to be. We ain't no ne'er do well with semi-colon piercings all over our body of text. When people are asked what they want to read, they might say poetry, but you know what they read when the browser is turned away is a good old fashioned flash fiction."

A nine hundred word family tragedy tilted back a shot of Jameson's and said, "And this guy ain't even a real poem. A real poem I can almost get behind. Especially the rhymers, they're good folk, but this guy is a prose poem. Not a story, not a poem. He's nomad writing. His passport is forged. Prose poem is the bastard child of classification. Me, I'm a slice of realism and that's the way it should be. The editors haven't figured me out, but a good publication will pick me soon and all those rejection jockies will just have to suck it."

The crime story said, "Yeah, and he's going to impress our women, and make them feel all arty. Leaving us here alone to sit, like we can't be attractive and desirable to a nice paranormal romance story."

The fable whispered, "But they ain't no women here. It's just us."

The prose poem got his drink and started going at it. "For work a thousand words or less, you guys sure natter on like a New Yorker article, never finished. Can you blame women for being more into me than you sad sack word jumbles? I have mystery, and I smell better."

The bartender mumbled, "Hey buddy, cool it with that kind of grammar. Maybe you be happier at the Haiku bar down the street, its a short joint, but they don't judge."

The prose poem took a drink of the gimlet, "Nah, I'm fine right here with all these beginnings, middles and endings. They got nothing for me to worry about."

The crime story pushed back from the stool. "That's where you're wrong you self-congratulatory paragraph!" Though drunk, he smoothly took out a sawed-off elliptical clause and pointed it at the prose poem.

The prose poem stood up and laughed. His smile shone like beams. He found strength in him like the tides. "Isn't that just like a flashie, bringing a clause to a metaphor fight." Like a waxing phase, the prose poem pulled out a sharp moon, one of the most deadly metaphors around. It was full like a belly, bright as a penny and mean as a hack writer having difficulty finding good similes. The bartender ducked behind the bar.

The crime story and the prose poem circled around each other, feinting and diving. All of a sudden, in walked a deus ex machina who looked at the ruckus and settled everything right. He revealed that the crime story and the prose poem were actually brothers, separated at birth by a follower of the William Burroughs cut-up technique. The two works embraced and swore fealty to each other. And soon, everyone in the joint was nominated for a Pushcart Prize.

The Cleansing

"This is the worst human sacrifice I ever been to," Billy said to no one in particular. He changed the angle of the hose to spray a part of the altar still covered in red gristle.

"Ah cool it," Mark said, "You're just peeved because there's a lot of blood today. Who knew the old lady was going to be such a geyser."

Billy turned off the hose and bent down to pick up the bleach bottle. "I don't know if that's it. No, that ain't it. I used to like this part. Sure it's the job, but I used to care about the cleaning. About the return to a pristine state, ya know. Back then, I was all, the more blood the better. But now, it's just the same ole crap. The cleansing bath, the donning of robes, the encircling, the chanting, the cheerful dancing after the knife. Man, every month. It's like watching reruns of a sitcom you used to like every night because that's the channel you always switch to."

"Wow man, that's some over-rehearsed speechifying, but hey, who am I to say anything about rote chanting." Mark tried not to laugh but found himself chuckling. "Oh, hey, Billy. I don't mean nothing by it. Just that I don't know if it's a good time to mention that you missed a severed toe over there, by the sconces. Don't want to bring down your righteous ire with mundane nonsense like evidence left at the scene."

Billy spotted the missing link and scooped it into the refuse bag. "That's a big old sacrilege. Thanks, Mark."

Mark turned on the ultraviolet to see if they missed any blood residue. "I would love to say I did it for you Billy, but you know, I did it for the group. Not for you. If you don't get that, well, I don't know, just breaks my heart to see you missing why we're here in the first place."

Billy sprayed down the spots that glowed under the light and decided to not speak any more. Mark was right, he was not for the group, he was negative. He was poisoning the group kool-aid, and not in the good way.

It was not long before the place was as it was before, perfect. It was time to go. Billy threw the refuse bags into the furnace and left without saying good-bye to Mark. What was there to say? He went out the side door and reached for his pack of Camels only to recall he didn't smoke any more.

"This was my first time, thanks." A small shadow spoke to him. A moment of acclimation let BIlly see the girl in front of him. She was there at the ceremony tonight. He thought he had noticed her.

"Well, yeah, I was there."

"I had no idea," the girl said. "I feel new. I feel better. You are the only one who hung around. I just wanted to say thanks."

Billy stopped wanting to smoke. He was being thanked. He was being blessed. "Well, its worth it. Just gotta remember that feeling every now and then, keeps you going."

The girl just smiled at him, having no idea what he was talking about.

Billy could only grin. "Hell, let me thank you. You remind me of things I can't believe I could forget. Come on. The night is still night, let's go for a ride."

The girl nodded and said, "To where."

Billy said, "To wherever, just as long as we drive fast, and if the gods are with us, we might hit a pedestrian. Come on, let's go do good works."

The Getaway

Soft Rock was post-coital and sweaty. He couldn't help it; he was, by nature, a great perspirer. He liked the jazzy feel of the bed he was lying in. This was good for an afternoon delight. Sky rockets in flight and all that falderall.

Soft Rock looked at the woman next to him. She seemed satisfied, but her face had the minor key shadings of disappointment, some atonal dissonance. This was something else he knew well on the faces of his afternoon dalliances. The woman leaned over and scooped up a pack of Pall Malls and lit up without offering him one. That was just fine, he wasn't focused enough to have that kind of pressing need.

"I didn't ask you at the wine bar," he said, "but I was wondering what your name is."

The woman spoke in a strong European accent that he didn't notice from before. "And why do you want to know something so useless?"

Soft Rock said, "I don't want anything. I'm not so forward or intent. I'm too accommodating for that. I was only but curious. Like wanting to know 13 down on a crossword puzzle I have no faith that I'll finish."

The woman sucked her cigarette, "If that is the case, I am a five letter word for roll out the music."

"Can you give me a letter?"

"First letter might be P."

Soft Rock swallowed; why did he have to mention crosswords? But then tumblers relaxed and he said, "Polka. You are Polka."

She nodded with a smirk on her face. "Remind me that if we ever meet again, to not have you help me with the Saturday Times Puzzle."

Soft Rock was satisfied that he was that clever to discover her secret. Of course she was Polka. It made logic: the rhythmic lovemaking, the old country gasps of possible pleasure. "Do you have a shower off the bedroom?" he asked.

Polka nodded and said, "Not for you." This was all right, this sheen of sweat and release was the closest Soft Rock was going to get to funky.

The sound came from below. It was the scratch of keys and locks. It was the heavy thud of boots on stairs. "My husband." Polka said it, but he was familiar enough with the script of this scenario that he could have jumped on her line and spoken it for her.

"I'm all about the window. Don't worry about me, I never break anything." He clutched his clothes and gave up his shoes for penance.

"No," said Polka, "I don't think I am worrying about you." The door burst open and there was a middle-aged man with torn jeans and bristle brush hair.

Soft Rock jumped out the window and landed like a legless cat. He only realized how scraped he was while he was running down the street. The guy, the husband, he knew him from town. It was Punk. Punk Rock. Same last name as him, but no relation.

He could hear the screaming as he turned the corner. He heard Punk shouting, "With him? You were in my bed with him?"

Soft Rock knew he had to stop soon to put on his clothes but he was too enamored of the running. He was a wanderer. Running on empty. Gone baby gone. Whatever that all could mean.

Directions for the Man in the Shirtsleeves Found in an Old Photograph, circa 1930

Look directly ahead. Be puzzled at the notion that someone is taking your picture. Grip the beer can in your left hand tight enough for the indentations to be noticeable from a distance. So many miles. So many years. Wear your hat at a high angle so that it does not shade your eyes. Squint from the sun or from habit. If your shirt is tucked in, be sure to pull out one tail. Fist up your right hand and hide it in your pants pocket. Purse your lips as if to ask why they are pointing that thing at me. Do not say it. Be paused. Be silent.

If you follow these directions, your soul will be lost forever. Your image will be stained and nestled for years in a box of vernacular photographs at a thrift shop. 2 dollars each. 3 for 5 dollars. You might be purchased and adhered into a collage. You might fade into grainy disregard.

Ten Lonely Rain Gods

The first lonely rain god sits on her bed and sings, "Cry Me a River." She looks up and says, "That's a joke. Cry me a river. That's a lot of tears. I'm a rain god. I was crying and so it's funny because, ah, forget it." She sings the song from the beginning, but not knowing all the words, hums most of it.

The second lonely rain god writes words on a dry erase board with a squeaky marker. He writes: draught, deluge, downpour, arid, sprinkle, giraffe. He pauses. "I just like writing the word. Giraffe. You try it. Giraffe. It's fun on the fingers as it slides into letters. Giraffe. Now try deluge. See. There is no fun in that word."

The third lonely rain god paces back and forth on the basketball court, mumbling to himself, "El Nino. El Nino. El Nino. Worst kind of false advertising I know. Little boy. Little boy. I created floods and storms and imminent destruction and they call me the little boy. Put me in short pants, pat my head and shove a chicklet in my mouth. El nino. Good boy. Go down to the basement fridge and get daddy another beer. My father did that to me once. I blocked the drains in the basement sink, and opened up the taps. I got daddy his beer and by the time they realized what I did, the basement was flooded and the house's structure was ruined. I'm nobody's El Nino."

The fourth and fifth lonely rain gods are in the rec room playing ping pong, Every volley echoes down the hall. They don't know what the score is. They don't know who is winning. "But I know who is losing," one of them says. "You can always notice the losers. Winners are tougher. Harder to see," The other one says, "Serve already. Stop making speeches." The serve hits the table like heat lightning. Eventually, the game is called on account of rain.

The sixth lonely rain god is working on a paint by numbers set. "Don't laugh," she says. "They're relaxing and they're popular. Maybe even hip. I said, don't laugh. You're breaking my concentration." She furrows her brow and carefully fills in a #14 spot with light magenta."But this one's defective. The box illustration shows Noah and the Ark and the two by two and all that propaganda, but that's not the picture I'm filling in. It's like a Mardi Gras parade or something with floats and beads raining down from balconies. I guess I can complain, but I'm too relaxed. Paint by numbers is relaxing."

The seventh lonely rain god, let's skip the seventh lonely rain god. It's for the best.

The eighth lonely rain god is sleeping. Or maybe he's pretending to be asleep. His ear buds are leaking out a meditation CD with the sounds of summer showers and crashing waves. Let's let him sleep, or let him continue pretending.

The ninth lonely rain god strums undiscovered chords on her boyfriend's guitar. She is humming. I'm sorry but the seventh lonely rain god is back and refuses to be passed over. I tried, but there she is in her bathrobe and mismatched fuzzy slippers. One foot is a teddy bear and the other is a porpoise. She is standing there giving that look she gives. The one that compels umbrellas to spontaneously open and slickers to tremble all through the building complex. She says, "Once entire nations worshipped me. They made bloody sacrifices to me. Sometimes I would deign to acknowledge their offerings with a humble shower. But now, they toss the runes of fronts and high pressure systems. Al Roker is a false god. The Weather Channel is a heretical temple."

The ninth lonely rain god has left. I suppose she couldn't hang around any longer. But where she was, is a piece of paper with some writing on it. It might be a poem. "The girl with the life preserver heart, is floating in the deluge. Her love is the wave crashing like persistence. Her hope is a chant. She shouts out adoration that cannot be heard. She wants to dry each other clean and blessed. They will release the livestock and live like Utnapishtim at the Mouth of the Rivers." That's what's written there. I guess some folks might call it a poem. I guess.

The tenth lonely rain god is pacing with the phone to his ear. They put him on hold and now he waits to speak to a supervisor. He's going to let them have it. Going to let it go, open up the floodgates. It will be wet and loud. But for now, he waits. And waits. And listens to the piped in music for those on hold: "Cry Me a River." .

The Quest of the Golden Cake

Good Afternoon, it was a pretty good day for him. He didn't have any aggression in class and did most of his work. The only incident was when he went to the bathroom in the afternoon. He's usually good about this at school. He was taking longer than usual so I sent an aid to check him and he was in the bathroom by himself, pushing his head into the mirror over the sink. He had to climb up to get to it. The aid got him down and he came back to the class, but we never saw him do this before. He was fine after that, just wanted to keep you abreast. Have a good night - G.

The Boy Who Was a Cat went into the dark room where he searched for the item he was on a quest for. The Great Leader had asked him to find the Golden Cake, which is not a cake to be eaten, but to worn like jewelry. The Ghost Enemy had stolen it and given it to one of his minions to keep. The Great Leader believed the Golden Cake aided him ruling the After Lands and he did not want that power to be near the Ghost Enemy. It did not matter if this was true to the Boy Who Was a Cat, all that mattered was that the Great Leader sent him on this mission, and that he trusted the Boy Who Was a Cat.

It took three days of hard travel through the Opaque Jungle and there were many adventures on the way, but the only thing worth reporting, and retelling to the Great Leader, was the Golden Cake. The Boy Who Was a Cat followed the trail to the Yellow Cave. The Dark Cat appeared and sneered at him, "You will never get what you search for! The Great Leader will never wear the Gold Cake. I have stolen it for the Ghost Enemy. You will have to go back a failure." The Dark Cat jumped back and went through a large oval mirror. The mirror rippled and the Dark Cat was gone.

The Boy Who was a Cat took out his sword and hesitated. Going through the mirror to the Dark Lands was a dangerous thing. The last time he went through, he thought only angry things for a week. But the quest was important and the goading of the Dark Cat would not stop him from what he needed to do.

He pushed the mirror with his sword and it opened like an eye and he squeezed through into darkness. The Dark Lands were certainly so. The Boy Who Was a Cat sang to his sword and it glowed enough light for him to move forward.

Soon he noticed something else glowing, he moved toward that and there was the Golden Cake. It also was bright, like the Great Leader himself. He went to it and scooped it up. He strapped it to his sash and headed back.

He walked for a long time, but could not find the back side of the mirror. Maybe that was why the Dark Cat left the Golden Cake for him to find, for he believed the Boy Who Was a Cat would not find his way back and be lost in the Dark forever. A vicious plan that was working. The Boy Who Was a Cat kept on turning and walking and walking and turning. The Golden Cake became heavy and weighed him down.

But it is important to remember that the followers of the Great Leader were never completely alone. And it came to happen that one of the Large Angels discovered him and took the Boy Who Was a Cat back to the place he needed to be. Everyone would soon be pleased with what he had done.

Dirt Bikes

My father was beside himself over the dirt bikes. A bunch of the neighborhood teenagers had dirt bikes and they rode through our subdivision late at night, every night. Because our house was on the corner of Hemlock Lane and Elm Street, they cut through our lawn, tearing up the grass every time.

His first course of action was talking to the dirt biker's parents. Did he really think that was going to help? It seemed that the ruts in the lawn got deeper.

Next, my father reasoned that he should make the lawn less appealing to the dirt bikers. He bought a large landscaping rock and placed it in the middle of the lawn, the place that the bikes always appeared to go through. In the morning, we woke to see that this large half ton rock was rolled up right next to the house. Like a giant Easter egg roll, they pushed the offending lawn obstruction away from their preferred bike path.

My father had the rock returned to its place and planted pricker bushes all around it. The bikers responded. The bushes were pruned down to the roots and the rock was now just gone, never to be seen again.

It was here that he stopped seeing them as annoying kids with dirt bikes and only as the enemy. He taught my sister and I a new word, proliferation.

From a Korean War buddy, he scored a half dozen or so landmines and as a family activity, we planted them in the lawn. It was similar to our gardening chores, if the geranium bulbs were hollowed out and filled with nitro glycerin.

We were awoken by two shattering explosions and pleas for help. No one was killed, but two of the kids were without dirt bikes and one was missing a pinky finger. That was the last time they tore through our yard.

The only thing, my father was not in ordinance back in Korea; he was a desk jockey. His ability to retrieve unused armaments probably was a tad underdeveloped. My sister discovered this fact as she ran through the yard for the school bus. She heard the distinct click of a landmine being stepped on.

She stopped and cried for help. She stood there for seven hours. They had to call the bomb squad from Chicago to deal with it. When she was finally taken off the mine, she had no more tears to weep. She was haggard and exhausted.

My father swept her into his arms and bombarded her with apologies. He was so sorry. How can he prove to her he was sorry? What can he get for her so she will forgive him?

My sister looked at him and said, "I want a dirt bike."

In the Pickling Fields

On the edge of the beginning, Moss Child crawled to the pickling fields for something to eat. This land was owned by the creators. The storytellers and cloth-spinners that chose to create this world, this beginning. They would not want her eating what was theirs, but Moss Child was hungry and hunger didn't stand on polite expectations.

With soft green fingers, she dug out the first jar that gravity and divine edict nestled under the earth. The jar was cast from the hide of old Gods. It was brittle and broke to the touch.

She took out the second jar. It was made from black ink. Inside she found a giant ossified heart. She gnawed at that organ for two days and stopped only when she thought she might tire.

She took out the third jar, made from the caul of infant stars. Inside were people, the we. She put one in her mouth, found it bitter and spit it out. She upended the jar and all the people tumbled out.

To their fleeing forms she shouted blessing, "Be free you bad food. Ruin the taste buds of those who should never have harvested you. Worship them, but never forget to get a decent wage for the adulation. Never be satisfied. When that happens, your flesh will mellow and taste sweet and they will greet you with smile and fork."

Moss Child found the other jars empty and went looking onto the next page for something new to please her.

Rodersangre

Rodersangre or Bebes du Vin- a large semi-aquatic rodent once found in lowland areas of Northern France. First documented in seventeenth century newspaper accounts, rodersangre or the Bebes du Vin resembled a nutria or painted tree rat. Their front teeth were sharp and gnawed tough vines. Herbivores, they lived on grapevines and grass.

Mostly considered to be pests, they were hunted and destroyed for centuries. It was only during the Great War, when the species was on the verge of extinction, that the potability of its blood was first realized. The blood of the rodersangre resembled wine in flavor, consistency and alcohol levels. Firsthand witnesses confessed it to be similar to young Beaujolais. Experts claimed the blood tasted of apple core, pine shavings and autumn heather.

The soldiers in the trenches kept captured rodersangre in their kitbags. The tradition was to kill them and drink the blood before going "over the top." Survivors stated that the blood gave them courage and they were not visited with hangovers from it.

American GIs enjoyed them as well, calling the rodents wine babies. As far as it can be discerned, the last verified rodersangre died soon after Armistice Day.

It should be noted that there was one further occurrence of the rodersangre in the literature. In 1922, Al Tuttleman, a WW1 veteran, opened a French restaurant, Mason du Eats, in Naperville Illinois that advertised "wine babies direct from the Old Country." He argued that because it was blood and not a fermented beverage, it would not fall under the Prohibition laws. An investigation discovered that these were not rodersangre but shaved woodchucks and the "wine baby blood" was grape juice spiked with wood alcohol. The restaurant was closed after three patrons lost their sight.

A Fairy Funeral

When the magical creatures dies. When the mythical folk bite it. When the fairies succumb to emphysema. When the trolls under the bridge perish from exposure. When the pixies get hit by the #5 inbound bus. When the men with the top hats put their wands up to their temples and blow their brains out. When the chalkline drawing does not hold the binding power to encircle and enliven, but only tells where the bodies fell.

Then it is time dress yourself in condolences. Adorn yourself with leaves and sod. Bedeck your body with charms and green ink tattoos. Make your presentations like dust. Like pepper. Like shawls. Like petals falling from the hands of prop masters hidden away in the scaffolding.

And walk into Black. This Black. This Darkness. It smells of patchouli and dusk. Feels like sandpaper lovers. Tastes of ocean's breath. Sounds of the pleadings of baby pterodactyls. This Darkness is infinite and geometric. There is an arc. There are parabola. There is a receiving line that snakes well past the door of forgiveness.

Some funerals are wailings and tears. Some are drinks and embraces. Some are good riddances and ravaged cheese platters. I am sorry for your loss. I lose for your sorrow. I am singing relief inside like Hosannas in the mosh pit.

At an enchanted funeral, there is no one to apologize to. Everyone is in the sarcophagus. You have to be prepared. You have to plan these things out. You have to write the will. Mapping out who will inherit the wealth. Who does the sky go to. Who gets the earth and the barrows. Who profits from the movie deals. Who get the magic. That's why we're here really. Who get the magic? Who gets the power?

Who will trick the unsuspecting now? Who mill make the unfathomable bargains to the hopeful now? Who will open the seams of existence and dance now?

Dance like yesterday's incantations. Dance like you're going to get some later. Dance like sweat and the Mozart baby in your momma's womb. Dance like fire and heat and consummation.

Be the flam. Be the blaze. Be the pyre. The ash. The phoenix. The wake. And for course. The next dance.

The Adjunct Professor of Cabbage

When I, in my role of Dean of the School of Economics, learned of the budget freeze, I was left with the task of cancelling several sections of beginning economics for the lack of an instructor. This would not do. So I decided as the other option, I would build one. One night, bolstered by single malt courage, I broke into the School of Agriculture's greenhouse and hurried back to my office with the building blocks for my faculty member.

I used hearts of romaine for the torso. Radicchio for the arms and endive for the fingers. Iceberg lettuce for the shoulders and upper legs. For the calves and feet, I utilized bok choi. I placed a large red cabbage on top of what I made and said that that was its head. Hearts of palm created the facial features, with pimentos for eyes. All that was left was to dress him in tweed and write up the syllabus for his new classes, and the new adjunct professor was instated.

The new instructor had three sessions of Introduction to Economics and two of the survey course: From Adam Smith to Modern Money Markets. Using the handout modules favored in personalized instruction systems, all the new professor had to do was sit in the front of class, while the students toiled away on the module assignments, and look stern. At this, the new adjunct professor excelled. Of course, the grading and course creation fell to the graduate teaching assistants. The TAs also had the added task of replacing parts of the professor when he wilted around the edges or when some fraternity prankster felt compelled to take a bite of his head.

At the end of the semester, I was pleased to learn that the new professor's students had higher-than-average test results and their course evaluations for their instructor were glowing. No one had a disparaging word for him. He was above reproach and leafy.

The other schools at the University noticed the success of this tyro educator and began to build adjunct professors for themselves. The comparative literature department had an instructor constructed of ramen noodles and soft pretzels. The Spanish department used varieties of sausages. The classics professor was composed of eggplant and red potatoes. The School of Asian Studies retired their adjunct professor made of kim chee when most of its students dropped the course in the first week.

Despite all these rivalries and jostling for prominence, none were as beloved as my economics adjunct professor of lettuce and greens. This was a great feather in my cap. Or so I thought. How these things happen in this cabbage-eat-cabbage world. I found myself dismissed from my job. My replacement? The very adjunct professor of which we speak. I created him like Pygmalion or at least a side salad.

I am sending out my CV to other universities, but I fear that I am not green enough in this new environment. A pinot noir cloud of despair shadows me, but at least it is dry and crisp.

I hear things about my former protégé. That he will not be satisfied in his current position. That his pimento eyes are not on the seat of the University President, but higher. The Secretary of Education in the cabinet of the President?

Who is to say how far a cabbage head can go in this world?

Lions

When the newspapers announced that lions were roaming around our hamlet of Marshville, Connecticut, the town fathers proclaimed that no children will play upon the streets, or even in the yards behind the houses.

Tree houses were erected with discarded driftwood wherever there were accommodating branches. All four of the Haversly boys fell off of their quickly constructed manse in one untimely motion by Jack Haversley. There were six broken bones shared between them.

The children of the tenement row threw over the pigeon coops on the roofs and drew hopscotch fields with chalk. They hung over the edge and jeered and sang at the men with the large nets driving around the streets in slow trucks.

Clothes lines were commandeered into monorail lines like in drawings we had seen of the Alps. Missy Meon often scurried to the center of one rope and dangled, her feet just inches from the ground. I still can hear her sing-song chant, "No lion's gonna get me. No lion's gonna get me. And me with tasty legs and toes. No lion's gonna get me."

My Aunt Loris looked after me, while my parents were still being searched for. She took me on outings on the telephone wires. We played tag and its bitsy spider until the sun brought us in for supper. Many times we just sat on the wires as she taught me cat's cradle. I would work the strings from her and squeal with success.

Aunt Loris wasn't too far removed from childhood herself. She wore fashionable hats and always made up new games. One Thursday morning she said, "Let's play Telephone Operator." She took out a telephone earpiece attached to a wire with a clasp. She attached the wire to the telephone wires we sat on and the two of us heard people talking.

"Now I might be mistaken, but that sure sounds like Mayor Wilson," she said with a smile.

We leaned in and listened. "Yes. You don't have to tell me this won't work for long. But what are we going to tell them? The truth? Better to say that's it lions and keep it at that."

Aunt Loris sat up, disconnected the clasp of the phone wire and said, "Let's get down from here. Let's kick off our shoes and run on the grass."

Of course, that's what we did. The feel of the grass between my toes was wondrous. I can still recall how it felt as we dashed away with no discernible destination

Charlie Minovitz

I know this guy, Charlie Minnovitz. He has gills on his neck. Tells me over bottles of Bud that he is no freak. Says that people are born with signs of waking dreams come true all the time. He can breathe underwater, but he never has. Living on Long Island, he's found a way to never see the ocean. He drives highways, visits shops by the off-ramps. Sends his kids to sailing class with his wife. Reminds her every time to make sure they got their life jackets on. He has a fear of the undertow that only a man who can breathe underwater can have. He always wears collared shirts, confesses his differences only here at this bar stool.

Charlie says he never tried his gills, but knows they work fine. Says you don't have to believe in your kidneys, but they believe in you. They work even without your prayers. He never takes a tub bath; he showers. Likes the force of the water hitting his skin. Likes to watch the water

spiral down the drain. He adds that he also loves to put up wet laundry on the backyard line to dry. Can spend the whole afternoon observing the process of evaporation.

His wife thinks he's crazy. Thinks it must be something with the gills. But now, after so many beers, he has no idea what it can be. He can swim under all the oceans, but that won't make him any more sober. He drains his bottle and wonders out loud how he's going to make it home tonight. He puts his head down on the bar and is asleep. Begins to snore evenly and loud. And I see the collar of his shirt expanding and contracting as if he was breathing from his neck. But I could be wrong. It could be a trick of the light. The lateness of the hour, and all the beers I am drowning in.

At the After School Program for Major Johnson Elementary

2:55 The girl with the Supergirl t-shirt and the frilly purple skirt runs into the after school program. She greets the afterschool teacher with her arms in front of her, flying as fast as her sneakers can go. "I'm a super girl. Not the Supergirl on TV because her show is on past my bedtime so I can't see her, but I am a super girl and I have fights and I rescue people from bad guys and I have arch enemies, and they are all girls too." She sprints past all the other children, assessing the risk level around the block area.

3:45 The super girl is saving the day. She is helping the kindergarten kid with the fire red cheeks and runny nose tie his shoelaces. The little kid thanks her and the super girl beams and flies off.

4:40 The super girl watches another child leave with their parent. She waves and tells them to do no crime. She is the last one here. There is no one else in the room. Just her and the afterschool teacher. The super girl stands with her legs out and her fists resting on her hips. If there could only be a superimposed American flag waving behind her, the image would be complete.

5:25 The cd playing Mozart for Kids stops and the afterschool teacher decides to not put in another disc. The afterschool teacher reflexively looks at her watch. She can't stop herself from mumbling, "Again. She's going to be late again." The super girl is in the art area pushing a crayon across a coloring page picture of pumpkins with forceful motions. She is not staying in the lines. She rips the paper with the force of her coloring.

6:05 The afterschool teacher leaves a message on the number she has for the super girl's mother. "Yes, hello. As you know, the final pick up is 5:30. I am calling again to see if there is any issue and please, if this number is not good, please supply me with a better one. Thank you." The super girl built a 12 block tower and is now pushing teddy bears off the top. At first, she was catching them as they plummeted, Now she only watches them slam onto the the carpet.

6:26 The super girl's mother is not happy with the attitude the afterschool teacher has. The mother was busy. Her car was giving her problems. She knows when she has to do pick up but crisis happens and her daughter understands. And no, she will not pay the fine for being late, how can she be expected to pay the fine for a bad car? The super girl gathers her bag and the art she made. She runs over to the afterschool teacher and whispers in her ear, "I am not the supergirl you know. I'm her arch enemy who looks just like her. I'm the Anti Super Girl. I'm in disguise. I'm pretending to be good. Don't tell anyone." As she crosses the room's threshold, the little girl in the supergirl t-shirt and frilly purple skirt turns and bestows on the after school teacher a large smile, full of teeth and knowledge.

A Walk in the Cities

One day Father Death and Father Life were walking hand in hand down the streets of the City. Which city? Well, sir, it was all cities all at once. It was London. It was Khartoum. It was Budapest. It was New Haven, Connecticut. Father Death and Father Life can do that kind of thing. And these two old gentlemen have spent many a lovely afternoon strolling together. But not recently. Work had been busy for both. The population boom completely exhausted Father Life. His hair turned gray and fell out completely. Father Death fared no better. With all the wars and diseases, his skin was now weathered like a rock face battered by the waves.

So this was the first time they had been out and about for ages. Father Life looked around the thoroughfare: at all the faces, pulses, and buzzing rhythms, and was filled with great pride. He turned to Father Death and said, "What do you say, old friend? These eyes. These breathing mouths. This throng of life. I would never say anything bad about you, but everywhere I go, I am greeted with the jubilation of existence." And Father Death chuckled and said, "Maybe that's true."

Well, sir, by and by, these two distinguished old men found themselves leaving the brightly lit storefronts and boulevards and into the shadowy, uneven streets that surrounded the commercial district. Outstretched hands dressed in tattered rags came out from crouching corners. People walked with lowered eyes, coughing into the air. Many asked for alms, for coins, for a little something for coffee. Father Death reached into his pockets and gave to everyone who asked. He had large pockets. They were filled with forgotten money, gold fillings, shawls for warmth, pennies off a dead man's eyes. His pockets were surely bountiful.

But Father Life reached into his pockets and found them bare. They were filled with promise, hope and growing potential. But nothing of substance, only a little lint.

And the sickly came to them and Father Life was ashamed. He could not find words for them. His tongue was hollow. But Father Death smiled and laughed and touched them with kindness. He gave them words to warm themselves. Like, "Not for a while, you still have time." Or, "You need to fight. There is fight in you still. I will not come for you until I have seen that you have fought." And to a few of them he just said, "Soon. I will come soon."

And as these things happened, Father Death and Father Life were on the boardwalk, by the river. Well, sir, Father Life was despondent and would not say a word for quite a while. Finally, he looked at his companion and said, "What good am I? I give life, but I can't help the needy. I have no comfort for the sick. Only in your palms is their any peace. Only in death is there any solace.

Father Death laughed. He said, "There is solace in me? Yes, I suppose there is. I am where the story ends. Yes. But the excitement comes from you. Only in living and experiencing what life offers, will they come to me with appreciation. I might be the final comfort, but you are all the simple joys. You are midnight kisses. You are light summer rain and birthday presents. You are home runs and pirouettes. You are crayon portraits, sad poems and meringue music. You are ripe tomatoes and leaps of faith.

"Every story must end in me, but you make the tale colorful. You give it a soul. No one would want to come to me if you did not fill them with the sights and sounds of this mad carnival. After a day at this parade, full of frights and thrills, everyone returns home, ready for sleep but filled with the knowledge that they have had a very fine day.

"Do not feel sad, for we are the mouth and the tail of the serpent eating itself." And Father Death took Father Life's face in his old hands and brought him to his lips, where they kissed by the running water. And kissed again.

And for one second, all of existence held its breath in a moment of unexpected harmony. And that's how it happened. Or at least, that's what I was told.

Watch Shop

It was the fourth watch shop window we stopped at as we headed to the movie. My brother always paused to look at the antique watches. " See that one, that's art deco design, that has the best workings." Each window was filled with old watches that I doubted worked. The windows were designed to be like a chocolate sampler box filled with surprise and precision. "That one," he said, "I need to check that one out."

"We're going to be late. Mom said you would take me to the movie. That means the whole movie." We were heading downtown to a revival house that was playing George Pal's The Time Machine. I had only seen it on our black and white TV when it aired late at night on Channel Nine's Million Dollar Movie. I couldn't wait to see what the Morlocks really looked like, all big and full of Technicolor.

"We're not late, and you've already seen it. You know how it goes. I really need to check out this watch." We went in and the place was tight and crowded. Only a handful of people could get into the shop at any moment. We were the only customers in there, but the guy behind the counter just kept working on some tiny springs coming from a rectangular watch.

After a minute of standing there looking at the man, my brother said, "Excuse me, but I saw the Elgin in the window. The one with the two tone case."

The man looked up and his eyes were small, pushed back way into skull. "Yes, the Elgin, it has the original band, little staining."

"I know, it's amazing. I was hoping to look at it. Check it out. See how much it is."

The man looked at my brother, at his sneakers and blue jeans. He looked at me, bouncing with anxiety. "Yes. It is a lovely watch." He returned his head to the watch he was working on.

We waited another two minutes and fifteen seconds. Then another thirty three seconds. The man kept working on the watch. "I want to look at the Elgin, please." Another twenty eight seconds. "Just because I don't look decked out, I can still be a customer."

Another two minutes and eleven seconds went by and I began hearing the tiny whirs and clicks of the watches surrounding me. "I can wait here all day," my brother said.

I looked up at him. "But the movie."

My brother didn't look at me. He just waited. His standing tall stance quavered and became unsteady. The man behind the counter leaned back and yawned.

In my mind, I began to play the beginning of the movie we were not watching. The lead actor announced to the other men that he had invented a machine that will allow him to travel in time. The men did not believe him. I saw it in beautiful color and swelling orchestration, though I still heard the thousand tick tick ticks of all things denied us. We were still at the watch shop. We were always at the watch shop. Time stopped. Time always does that.

Mashugana Christmas

Santa was too drunk to go down the chimney, instead he barreled through the side door of the rec center of Temple Beth Israel Retirement Village. The women were playing mahjong. The men were pretending to concentrate on their game of hearts. But instead were checking out Mrs. Gold, the new arrival at the retirement village. She was fine with short hair. Zaftig with hips.

The air conditioner was fighting an unseasonable May afternoon, when Santa threw his body head first into the room with hearty good cheer. His suit was stained the color of brick seen at midnight. His beard was yellow more than white. "Ho Ho Ho! Who's been good little boys and girls?"

"Hey Santa Wrong Year, I haven't been a boy since 1935."

"Oh really Murray Myers, so when exactly did you become a man?"

"Hey Santa, wrong month. It's May."

"Hey Santa, wrong time of day. Has your wish list gotten so large that you are only getting to us now?"

"Hey Santa, wrong faith. Check the address. Jewish. Nursing. Home."

Santa was confused. Staring distantly towards something, perhaps to the North Pole. He spoke with words full of passion and whiskey scented spittle. "There is no wrong faith," he said. "Every child needs Santa. If there is a need or poverty, there is Santa. A present for just being a child. Acceptance in the form of a Barbie doll or a Tyco train. No child should forget that."

"We're not children anymore."

Santa raised his torn canvas bag in front of him, as if it were a final defense. "No one isn't a child. To me you are all rosy cheeked cherubs who want dolls and trucks."

"Maybe if that truck was a Ford Explorer, then that Santa can earn himself a drink."

And suddenly, taken with the spirit of the season, the rec room shouted out their want list to this Santa Claus

"A well behaving bladder."

"A high yield retirement fund."

"A viagra free boner."

"Peace in the middle east, kennehura."

"A good tasting bagel, remember when they had taste?".

"Me? I just want my grandkids to call."

And there was a pause, which turned into a silence, and then a quiet moment of agreement. And Santa wobbled forward, his head peering into his bag, unsure if anything in there would fit the measurement of the request.

Esther Hegelman cleared her throat, "Mr. Claus. You have a lot to answer to us Jews, to us grandparents on a budget. Our children put up Christmas trees because Hanukkah is not flashy enough. It's a pitzelah holiday. You make our kin sing carols at school. And watch on the television Rudolph and his nose. You could not destroy us through pogroms or holocausts, But now we are buried in wrapping paper and Andy Williams Christmas Specials."

Santa straightened up as much as he could, "My dear madam, I am beyond Christian. I was appropriated by them. I am of the earth."

"You are of the bottle," a voice rang out.

"No!", he shouted. "Earth!" And he fell broken like a box of ill fitting toy parts. And as the security guard was called, Santa Left. Departed. We cannot be more specific.

Mr. Hemmel saw him escorted by security.

Several others swore that he went up the chimney, though there is no chimney in the rec room.

But with all that said, nobody changed. No one converted. No one truly believed that he was anything other than a deluded drunk.

,

Still, the new woman, Mrs. Gold, agreed to go to a movie with Mr. Aaron Fischer. Albert Blish found a bottle of schlivitiz in his room, the very kind his father drank when he told tales of Russia. And Sylvia Moskowitz's granddaughter called, just to say hi. No, it was not a day of miracles. But it was a day where something happened. And sometimes that is miracle enough.

Performance Art in the Age of the Zombie

Grant money is no longer available for artists to finance their work, (what with no governments or set monetary systems, and the general threat of being bitten by members of your audience), but that does not stop several artists from creating pieces that speak to their world.

An old school performance artist stated, "This isn't different from Before. Doing this kind of work is never wanted, but that does not mean its unnecessary" She captures zombies and dresses them up in themed costumes and then sends them back into the infected zones. Her piece, "Send in the Clowns," where she dressed 300 zombies to look like Bozo the Clown, is still discussed. She reports children across the safe zones wake up screaming from dreams of ravenous Bozos. The artist considers this a successful result.

Another artist makes a show of eating the flesh of zombies in his piece, "Turnabout Cuisine." He butchers and prepares the flesh of neutralized zombies in traditional Japanese shabu shabu style, dipping a thinly sliced sliver of Zombie into a bowl of boiling water long enough to burn away contagion and make it delicious. In lieu of an exhibition catalog, he offers a zombie cookbook for sale. In the past two years, he has sold twelve copies. "It's becoming a movement," He says, "It's the next new thing."

One art collective, the Undead Duchamps, put on a show called "sneak attack," where, in the middle of the night, they dressed themselves as zombies and pretended to attack zone citizens.

As with some art pieces, they did not get the expected results. It goes without saying, this piece was performed only once. The survivors of the collective recall the performance warmly.

The artist who created the zombie piñata piece has been embraced by several safe zones, with offers inviting her to present the piece elsewhere. She has declined the chance to continue with the work, saying, "It's a hard piece to perform. First you have to capture a zombie, then you need to open up its belly, fill it with candy and sew it back. I take pride in my needle work, it is one of the important aspects of the piece, So, I don't skimp there. Then I need helpers to truss it up and hoist it over the compound. The general public really loves this work. You can see the joy on their faces when the candy is released. But there is more to me then this one performance. I'm not just the lady who beats the candy filled zombie with a stick.

I am so much more. I am only just beginning my artistic journey."

One artist performed a piece entitled, "Transformation-Infestation," in which he let a zombie bite him. He then sat in a lotus position as he calmly waited for the typical metamorphosis. The crowd was surprisingly thick as they watched the slow change occur. When the artist was burned away and all that remained was the zombie, the Zone Leader went over and cut off its head. The artist had prepped the Zone Leader in advance to say, "I don't know art, but I know what I like," when he cut down. For some reason, he didn't say that. He trailed off, as if distracted. He said, "I don't know. I just don't know."

Two Figures with Crows

Witness with me: two sisters wrapped in black, standing upon the snow, and a murder a crows.

There are two sisters in the snow, rigid and still. One has a profile face. The other does not have a face at all. Her back is to us, always away from us, and a murder of crows.

The two sisters wrapped in black, standing upon the snow are twins completely identical. You can only tell them apart by the fact that one of them does not have a face. Her back is to us, always away from us. They are called Dark Hollow and Hollow Dark. They have names. All creatures standing on the snow have names, and a murder of crows.

There are two twins you can tell apart for one is whispering an aviary augury. That is Dark Hollow. She is counting crows.

"One for sadness. Two for mirth.

Three for marriage. Four for Birth.

Five for laughing. Six for crying."

She pauses in the cold. The jet trails of her breath pass like smoke before her like untended thoughts. She does not ask her sister what number she would need to count to before the rhyme would include anything like them and their harvest.

"Seven for sickness. Eight for dying."

She does not ask her sister if they will be counted, while they stand rigid

but still harvesting the crop.

"Nine for silver. Ten for gold."

Why do they cultivate the crop? Why do they reap? Bleed and bend and never move.

"Nine for silver. Ten for gold.

Eleven. A secret that never will be told"

and a murder of crows.

There are two sisters wrapped in black, standing upon the snow. Hollow Dark turns from the camera gaze of unseen observers at an underheated museum. Unseen observers, like you and I and a murder of crows.

Hollow Dark stops harvesting. I think she stops harvesting. It is hard to determine when she is harvesting, and when she is still and remembering her Norse Mythology. Tales of Odin-All-Father she heard in a classroom. Hollow Dark says out loud: "Once Odin-All-Father had crows as familiars but forsook them for the raven. The raven was sleeker, and had better PR representation. But the crows liked the perch high up on all father's shoulder, and refused

the demotion, staging a work stoppage. So, Odin decided to eat them all. He cooked one crow in an earthen pot he buried in embers. Its meat fell from the bone and Odin called that dish Halo. He swallowed the next whole. It flapped down his throat and he called that one Mother. He pickled three in different brines, and called them Bluster, Terrible and Finger. The rest flew

away, not wanting to be eaten. Or named. Is it any wonder that we call a gathering of crows a murder? Is it any wonder that when I see them I am empty and famished?"

Dark Hollow turns not at all to her sister and says, "You told that one before. You tell me that one every time before." and a murder of crows.

There are two sisters wrapped in black, standing upon the snow, freezing their wills against each other.

-I am tired of your counting Dark Hollow (and sadness)

-I am tired of your All-Father stories Hollow Dark (and mirth)

-I hate your half moon profile Dark Hollow (and marriage)

-I hate your faceless anonymity Hollow Dark (and birth)

-I hate your insistence on the toil of the harvest Dark Hollow (and laughing)

-I hate your insistence on the toil of the harvest Hollow Dark (and crying)

-I am cold (sickness)

-I am empty (dying)

-I am lonely (silver)

-I am lost (gold)

-But the harvest.

-But the harvest.

Yes, the harvest (a secret that will never be told) and a murder of crows.

Witness with me: two sisters. In black. In snow. Aren't you shivering for them? Aren't you weeping for them and faceless? There were once explanations. Of course, there were explanations. But then, there was once a sky behind them. It is dark void now. The sky is completely is completely dark with approaching crows. Dark. And hungry. And never to be told.

Wonder Woman

Wonder Woman watched the business lady's kids. Don't ask her what the kids' names are. The names are ridiculous. Unpleasant to the tongue. Courtney. Ashley. Adrian. Poisonous, numbing. When the business lady is out of ear shot, she bestows the children with proud Amazonian names. The names of goddesses. She sings them lullabies stolen from her mothers. She wipes their mouths. Their behinds. She fold the pants and bibs. She vacuums the crumbs, sponges away the throw up. She sits with the children in the front room. She tells them to, "Look out. Look outside. My airplane is parked in the yard." The children shout, "Where, we don't see any airplane." Wonder Woman says, "It's right there. You can't see it because it's invisible." The children squeal and clap, as if this was a game.

Heist Genesis

In the beginning there was the Alarm, clarion birth. Ear shattering and fierce. The alarm brought Panic, which was what they called the world. It also brought the Po-lice, which is what we call the Law of the Man. Yes, the Po-lice formed from the clanging need of the Alarm and went to shake down informants, backtalk the press and track down clues that would bring them to the Prime Suspects. They were looking for them, the Crime Twins: Aid and Abet.

Aid and Abet had stormed the Bank of Blessings. They popped the tills, filled the bags and split fast. They split fast, but Abet, who was never as fleet of foot as his brother, tripped over the Eye of Security and brought Alarm. As they fled the First Crime Scene the Po-Lice squeezed one off and hit Aid in the leg. Despite the gimp leg, Aid and Abet kept barrelling down blind alleys.

"Brother," Aid said to Abet, "you must ditch me. Leave me to the Law of the Man."

Abet listened and said, "Nuts. We are twins. We are brothers. We rob together. We bleed as one. We will escape as one. So cool that dime novel doom talk and let's find us a Holing Place."

Aid looked about him, at this new land of distress. This landscape of pawnshops and fake ID hawkers and said, "I know this place. I know this place like it has always been mine. I got an old lady near. We can hole up there."

And so they went past streets and over winos until they found the coldwater flat of Aid's Old Lady. They banged up one flight of stairs and rested. Aid bled on the landing and that first pool of blood gave us greed. They banged up another flight of stairs and rested. Aid bled on the landing and that pool gave us lust. They banged up a third flight of stairs and rested. Aid bled on the landing and that pool gave us jealousy. They banged up the fourth and final flight and rested. Aid bled on the landing and that pool, the Fourth Pool. No one knows what the Fourth

Pool gave us, but even today, when one of us is taken with itchy neck and does something rash and hard we say that that sumbitch has bathed in the Fourth Pool.

At the fourth floor, they reached high enough up the building to go to ground. They knocked six times before Aid's Old Lady answered. She saw what was there at the threshold and said, "Aw damn. The hell you two want?"

Abet said, "We need a place of holing."

Aid's Old Lady said, "Not a chance even with fixed dice. All you do for me is bring the Heat down on my ass."

The dying Aid said, "Then let us be warm at least. Let the Heat come. Let us be blazed pure, to be shown blue white hot. The Heat will always be on our heels. It is just a question of where the fire will embrace us."

Aid's Old Lady did not budge. "Whatcha got in the bags?" she asked.

Abet lifted up the first tote. "This bag has Peace that we stole from the Bank of Blessings." He picked up the second tote. "This second bag has all the Paradise the Bank had in its vaults. Do you want to see?"

Aid's Old Lady shook her head no. She said, "Come on then. You're messing up my doormat."

She gave them beer and chips. She played music from the radio. She gave them chairs to sir silent upon. Aid looked at his brother and said. "I die. I die. I'm the busted perfect crime. I'm the rat in the room with the light bulb and I can't help myself from singing. I die, brother. I die. I will see you again in the Safe Place." He closed his eyes and slumped his head to his dead heart and was no more.

Abet was not awarded a chance to wail grief because the Po-lice were pounding at the door. "Open up. We have you surrounded." Abet looked towards Aid's Old Lady and said, "Do you have a way out?"

She said, "Natch. You always have to have an Escape Route." Which is still true to this day, friends.

Abet gave Aid's Old Lady the two bags of stolen goods and said, "Scram. I'll catch up with down the road and it even." And Aid's Old

Lady took the bags and scrammed. The front door exploded into shards and the Po-lice swarmed at the threshold. Abet blazed with lead and righteousness.

He took one in the chest. He spurted out life. He fell onto the body of his brother and they fused together into hard metal. The metal was so dense it crashed through all four floors of the apartment and pushed down into the center of the world. Wherever we tread, the Crime Twins are always underfoot.

The Authorities never found Aid's Old Lady or the bags of Peace and Paradise. But that, friends, is why we gather in this Safe House. We bring offerings of swiped food, picked pockets and jacked cars to the memory of Abet and Aid. One day, one day, we will go to the next place where Aid's Old Lady will greet us and present us with the stolen goods of the Bank of Blessings and only then will we at last stop running and get our fair share

Under the Sign

We lived under the sign of carburetor. E slept in rooms behind the shop. We bade carburetors grow up right. What else could we do, living under the sign we did?

My brother loved a girl who lived under the sign of comb and scissors. They ran away down the street and settled in a storefront with a sign of a paint can over it. They sell paint. They blend their own colors with clay and berries from the fields and mix it with a yard stick they bought from my cousin, who lives under the sign of the ruler.

My older sister took shelter under the sign of the red shoes. Mother shushes us when we mention her.

My younger sister became angry and movie in with the other angry people under the sign of the clenched fist.

This left me the only child with mother and father under the sign of carburetor. But fuel injection and dust orphaned our business and we became lonely for custom.

I went North for work. I live under a sign of stars. Staring up, I wonder what shapes they form. What wonderful thing are they advertising? What dreams are they selling for me now.

Green

"We can go anytime, sir," I say. "Put the ball in the cup, call it a scratch."

He looks up from his club towards my voice. "Who's that? Who said that?"

Was it stupid question day at the country club? "It's me, sir," I say with an unexpectantly squeaky voice. "It's your caddy, and we're past double boogie. Push it in the cup and we can go to the next hole."

The golfer looks almost at me. "My caddy? Tell me, is the ball in the hole?"

"No, sir. It's about fifteen feet to the north."

"So I'm on the green."

"Yes, sir."

"Then maybe in a pesky sand trap?"

"No, sir."

"Then I must have some pissed-off club member right behind me waiting for me to finish."

"No, sir. I believe you were the last party to leave the club house. It's quite dark right now."

"Damn straight. I don't need much light. I can feel the ball. I can sense the shots. Who needs eyesight?"

Is it Obvious Question Day at the country club? I want to say, yes. Yes, eyesight is a good asset for a golfer, you blind freak. Boy, do I hate being the newest caddy and getting stuck with you. But the Angel of Good Tips lands on my shoulder and I say, "Absolutely not, sir. All it takes is skill. You are on the green after all."

"You got that right," he says. "I'm on the green. Don't need nothing but ability. Diabetes can't take me off the green, can it?"

"Not a chance, sir. It's your shot."

"Watch how it's done." He hacks at the ball and it meanders several feet past the hole. "How'd I do, boy? Did I make it? Are we done with this hole?"

Are we done with this hole? Is it Unanswerable Existential Question Day at the country club? No, sir. We will never be done with this hole. We will be stuck on this green panacea like purgatory until celestial trumpets herald the end of our sentence. Chip it to heaven, sir. Chip it to heaven.

Perhaps we shouldn't leave this green. This green is home-base. It is olly olly oxen free. On this green you haven't lost your sight to diabetes. On this green I am not your little snot boy for tips. On this green we surely must be blessed. Here it is Elysium Fields. It is HyBrasil. It is Eden. It is getting darker and darker.

I should tell him he made the hole. I should tell we're done. I should tell him.

But I find myself leaning on the 8th hole flag saying, "No, sir. You missed. But you'll get it next time. I'm sure of it. You'll get it next time."

He smiles. "Yeah," he says, "this broken body ain't licked." The sun has set and he swings one more time, for salvation.

67 Mustang

For this story, you need to understand one point; the car is real. Everything else is made-up. When I look back and decide not to tell this story, the only thing I cannot rearrange is the car. More solid than memory. Built Ford tough. The car was old even then. Older than my seventeen years. My name is unimportant. The girl. Her name is not clearly recalled. But if I did remember it, I would give her a false one. The car refuses to be anonymous. It was a maroon, '67 Mustang. Hard top. Lead gas. Automatic transmission. Fading chrome. It had the amenities of a monk's chamber: steering wheel, gas pedal, four tires, engine. Do you need anything else?

In that car, 0 to 60 was a figment of the imagination (just like the rest of this story). It lived on the edges of the respectable. It only breathed properly when air was pounding at 65 miles an hour or harder. The back window was epoxied shut. The moorings of the passenger seat were broken, so that it moved back and forth like a rocking chair. Every miniscule pothole was a lesson in seismic activity. And the girl, sitting in the rocking chair passenger seat, was thrown up and down. Seatbelts were present, but didn't click shut. This was never about safety. This was about appearance. In this car, even I had the appearance of factory finish good looks.

We were beautiful. A complete fashion makeover as provided by Detroit Motorworks. We were beautiful, and Icarus was my co-pilot.

I was gripping the steering wheel, pointed home. It was time to go home. We were trying to end the day as quickly as we could. The car was happy to oblige. Out of the three of us, it was the only one talking. The rumble of engine. The hiss of tire on asphalt. It singing the song of freedom and future.

We were not listening. We were wrapped in our moment of conclusion. Planning how we would rewrite this moment. Make it imaginary.

The girl and I played with words at her doorway. We'd call each other soon. And then I was at the reservoir, sitting on the car's hood, chucking stones into the dark void of water I believed was in front of me. Not hearing nor recalling them hitting the skin of the lake.

Memory is a V8. With age, the pistons will misfire. The girl is gone. The story I have not told is gone. And some days I am sure that I am gone. A piece of adolescent fiction. But 67 Mustang. Full of substance and motion.

We are the tales we do not tell each other. Everything is negotiable. But the car is always real.

Dave, the writer of these things, talks about this book

If you were one to read my work in online magazines and small journals around 2007 to 2013, I am sure you might have purchased this book to read once more the story "Mrs. Greenthumb's Garden." You read it years ago and figure it will be in here. I am sorry to disappoint. That story is well and truly gone. It was published, but it ain't here no more. It ain't anywhere. It might as well not have been written.

That last paragraph is in jest. No one was waiting to reread that story. I do not remember it at all. Not one bit. It's in the "Published Stories" spreadsheet I diligently kept. It has the name of the story and the magazine (or e-zine or whatever it was) that accepted it. And that's it. It is not attached to any email. It is not in any hard drive that I was wise enough to back-up. No. I can't find anything online about the magazine that published it. Did it publish it? I have no clue.

I spent a fruitless hour searching my files and the internet for this lost marvel. Lost marvel, indeed. If you have read some or all of these stories, you will know that there were no gems hidden away here. Just stories. Some better than others. But still, I was hoping to find "Mrs. Greenthumb's Garden" and be amazed and astounded. There is nothing like be reacquainted with your own work, like it is a stranger off the street.

For that period of time, I sent out a lot of short, brief stories to be published. Most of them were for e-magazines and journals. Some were in books and real magazines. But most of them were published in little websites. Nothing wrong with a little literary web site. I loved them all. And most are gone. They have given up their claim on their little parcel of world wide web real estate and everything is past tense. I got about 125 stories published in that time. Only a handful can still be found online. Some can be found through archive.org, but some are just no more.

I decided a couple of days ago to find some of my old pieces and put them in an e-book. Much of my output had a fable like feel. Or there was a strong flavor of magic realism. I decided to focus on these. A few of the stories were never published, but I still remembered them, and liked them enough to include. I hope you enjoyed the stories that you read. I hope you didn't read them all in one sitting, that might be a little too much to handle. But sample them. Take a sip or two. Be satisfied with how many you decide to try.

Acknowledgements

Wing Mending was published in Every Day Fiction

Several Ways to Woo a Lady with the Aide of a Ball Peen Hammer was published in Black Scat Review

Sleeves was published by Post Card Press

Breaking Down Lions was published by Fickle Muse

The Loud and the Silence was published in Fickle Muse

Traffic Signs You Might Come Across was published Smashed Cat Magazine

Leaders was published in Weird Year

Freeze Tag with Jack was published in Moon Drenched Fables

Millennium Locks was published by Weird Year

The Church of the Frankenstein Monster was Published by Skive Magazine

Artistic Necessity was published by Abeleon Literary Journal

Poetry Night was published in Binnacle Literary Journal

At the Slush Pile Saloon was published by RadiusLit

The Cleansing was published by the Beguiling

The Getaway was published by Every Day Fiction

Directions for the Man in the Shirtsleeves was published by Mudluscious

10 Lonely Rain Gods was published in the Deluge Anthology

The Quest of the Golden Cake was published by Yesteryear

Dirt Bikes was published by Linguistic Erosion

In the Pickling Fields was published by Linguistic Erosion

Rodersangre was published in Le Scat Noir Encyclopaedia

The Adjunct Professor of Cabbage was published in Every Day Fiction

Charlie Minovitz was published in Every Day Weirdness

At the After School Program for Major Johnson Elementary was published in Every Day Fiction

A Walk in the Cities was published in Every Day Fiction

Watch Shop was published in Pound of Flash

Performance Art in the Age of the Zombie was published in the anthology Aim for the Head

Wonder Woman was published in November 3rd Club

Heist Genesis was published in Every Day Weirdness

Under the Sign was published in Mudluscious

Green was published in Every Day Fiction

67 Mustang was published by Every Day Fiction

About this Book

Santa Claus comes in roaring drunk at the Jewish Nursing Home.

Father Death and Father Life walk hand in hand down the streets of the city.

A variety of performance artists practice their calling during a zombie apocalypse.

There is the creation of the universe as seen as a film noir heist.

A church worships the Frankenstein monster as the savior.

"Not a Day of Miracles" is a collection of brief tales. None of them lasts long enough to question them. They are funny, wry fables based on bits and pieces of many parts. Poetic and ridiculous. They will entertain.

About the Writer

David has written over 30 e-books. They are all available wherever you purchase such things. He has written novels, short story collections, memoir and books in pop culture studies. He runs a weekly poetry reading in Worcester, Massachusetts. He has been involved in spoken word events for over 20 years. A lot of the stories collected in this book were originally written to be read at these open mics. He also is the editor of a monthly e-zine, The Long Weekend Review, which publishes small books where the chosen writer has absolute freedom, as long as the entire thing is written with-in 72 hours. He ran a blog where he attempted to go to every bar in Worcester and have a gin and tonic there. There are two Gin and Tonics Across Worcester e-books about the ordeal.

<u>Short Story Collections:</u>
Tales from the Re-animators Saloon
Reynold's Home for Retired Time Travelers
The Madre and Gander Employment Agency
The Final Girl Support Group Annual Brownie Bake-off and Other Stories
The Further Adventures of Polly Mintslab
<u>Short Novels:</u>
More Sopping Products
Funny Animals
77 Unnamed Love Gods
The Truth Seeker
Well Remembered Movies
<u>The Pop Culture Books</u>
Mama Cass's Golden Caramel Bar (about one episode of the New Scooby Doo Movies)
Are You a True Life Form? (about the Perry Rhodan SF novels)
In This Reality (a look at a single Tom Petty music video)
macphersondavid607@gmail.com

David Macpherson is a Writing Stuff is his Facebook page.
Find him at instagram at davidscottmacpherson
He blogs at 100pagedash.wordpress.com

* 9 7 9 8 2 2 4 8 2 2 8 1 2 *